A JOB FOR BUZZ

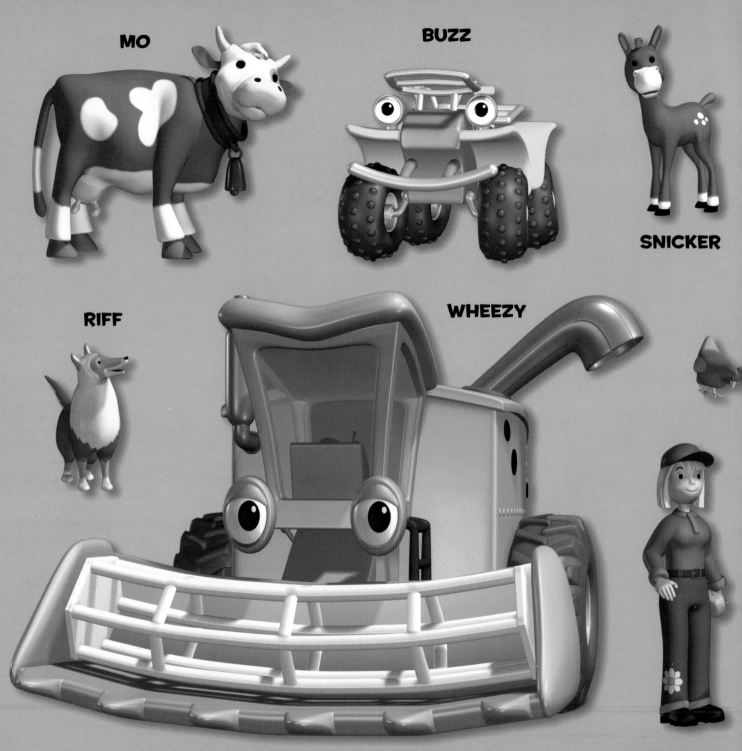

MO

BUZZ

SNICKER

RIFF

WHEEZY

FARMER FI

THE SHEEP

WACK

BACH

THE HENS

PURDEY

REV

TOM

WINNIE

MATT

First published in Great Britain by HarperCollins Children's Books in 2004

3 5 7 9 10 8 6 4 2

ISBN: 0-00-718903-6

Text adapted from the original script by Mark Holloway

The Contender Entertainment Group
48 Margaret Street, London W1W 8SE

Tractor Tom © Contender Ltd 2002

A CIP catalogue record for this title is available from the British Library.
Printed and bound in China

A JOB FOR BUZZ

An imprint of HarperCollins*Publishers*

It was a busy day at Springhill Farm. Tom and Fi had lots of jobs to do.

Buzz was very keen to help, but every time he did he got in the way. When he tried to stop Mo eating the hay, he almost crashed into Tom!

"Buzz!" cried Fi. "This work is too difficult for you. Leave it to Tom."

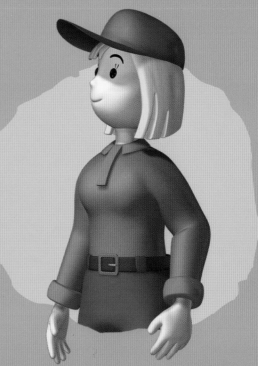

That night, Buzz was very cross that he hadn't been allowed to work at all.

Tom got all the best jobs on the farm.

Buzz didn't like this so he came up with a very naughty plan...

The next day Farmer Fi was up bright and early to get Tom, "Come on, Tom. It's going to be another busy day," she called.

But Tom's engine wouldn't start. Fi had a lot of work to do. What was she going to do without Tom?

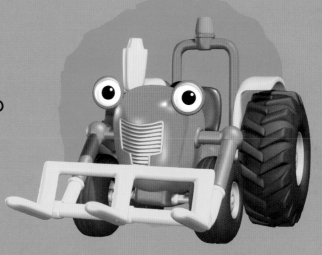

Buzz rushed up. "Do you think you can do Tom's jobs for today?" Fi asked.

But Buzz couldn't pull the trailer because it was too heavy. He couldn't move the sheep because they played tricks on him.

And when he tried to move the bales of hay he nearly had an accident!

"It's no use, Buzz, you just aren't strong enough," said Fi.

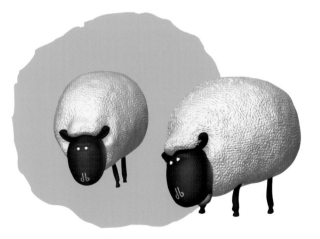

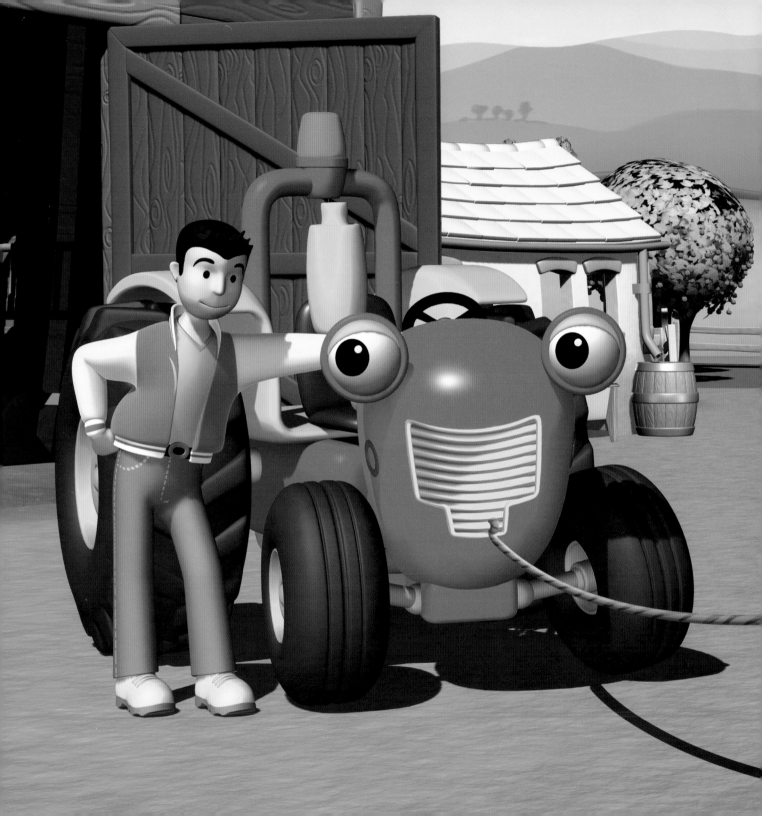

Matt was trying to work out what was wrong
with Tom.

He asked Rev to pull Tom to the top of Beckton
Hill so they could bump start him.
Tom was worried.

"Hey, don't worry,"
laughed Matt. "It is a
great idea and it's
bound to get you
working again."

When they got to the top of Beckton Hill Rev thought he would give Tom a helping hand.

Suddenly, Tom started to roll down the hill! Faster and faster he went.

Over the bridge and into the farm, where he crashed into the hen house!

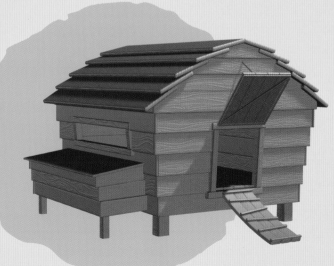

Back at the field Fi could hear one of the hens
calling and went to look.

"Oh, no!" she cried. It was stuck in
some brambles.

Fi tried to help the hen, but she got caught in
the brambles too.

Buzz tried to free Fi, but he couldn't do it.

"It's no good," she said. "Go and get Tom!"

So Buzz rushed off to the barn to get Tom.

"What's wrong?" asked Matt "Has something happened to Fi? Tom can't help, he's still broken."

Buzz raced towards Matt and lifted him off his feet, then carried him to the hen house.

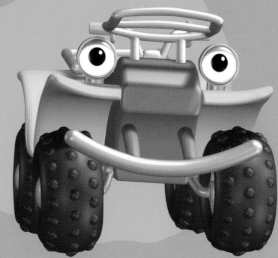

"What are you doing?"
shouted Matt.

"Is there something in the hen
house?" Matt looked inside the hen
house and found a piece of Tom's engine.

"How did this get here?" he asked. Buzz looked
guilty.
"Never mind, at least we can fix Tom now," said
Matt.

Matt and Buzz fixed Tom, then Tom went to rescue Fi.

"Thanks for mending Tom, Matt," said Fi.

"That's ok," replied Matt. "I had some help from Buzz, but I think he might have had something to do with Tom breaking down in the first place."

"Bu-zz!" said Buzz, apologising.

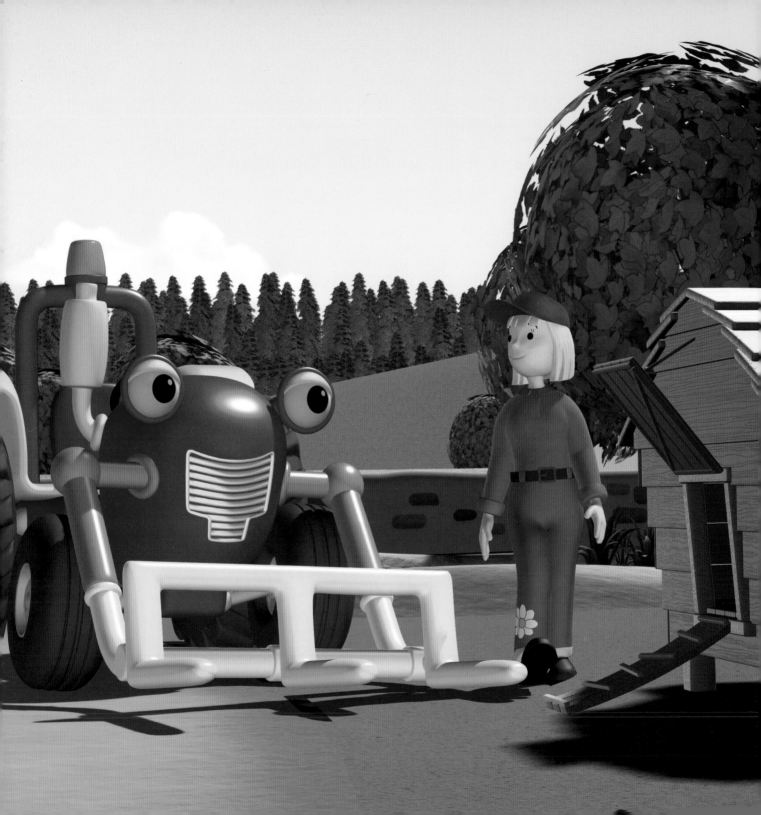

Tom and Buzz were soon very busy doing a whole days work.
"Well done," said Fi. "What would we do without you, Tom?"

As Tom went off to the barn Buzz tried to follow him. "Where are you going, Buzz?" called Fi. "I have got one more really important job especially for you!"

Fi knew Buzz had only been
naughty because he wanted
to feel as important as
Tractor Tom, so she gave him
a very special job to do.

"Stopping the sheep from
causing trouble is one job
that he's just right for,"
smiled Fi.

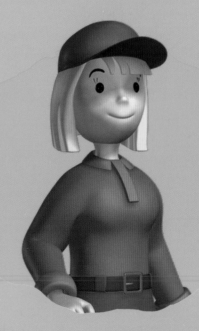

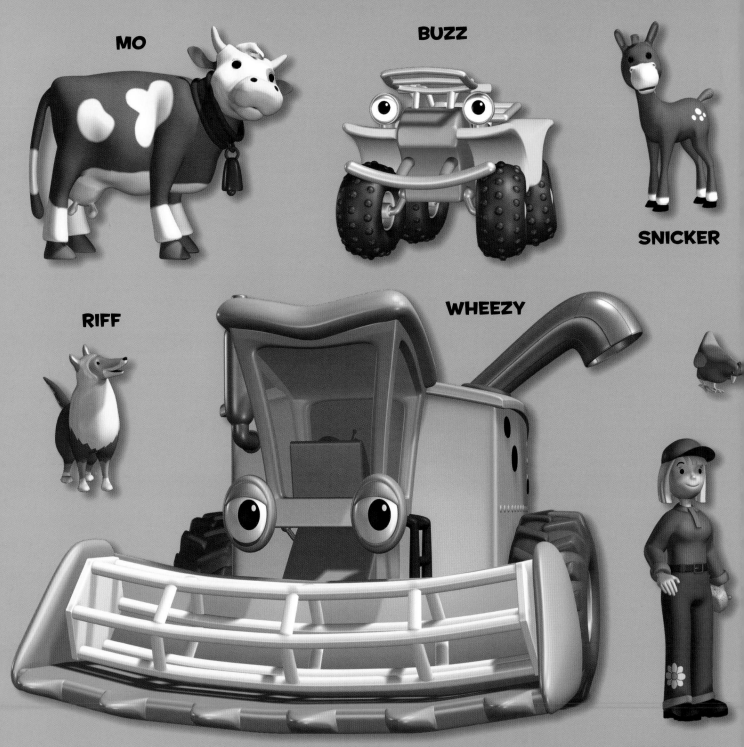

MO

BUZZ

SNICKER

RIFF

WHEEZY

FARMER FI

THE SHEEP

WACK

BACH

THE HENS

PURDEY

REV

TOM

WINNIE

MATT